ZOMBIE STORIES
TO SCARE YOUR SOCKS OFF!

EDITED BY BENJAMIN BIRD

raintree
a Capstone company — publishers for children

Raintree is an imprint of Capstone Global Library Limited, a company incorporated
in England and Wales having its registered office at 264 Banbury Road, Oxford, OX2
7DY – Registered company number: 6695582

www.raintree.co.uk
myorders@raintree.co.uk

Designed by Kay Fraser and Tracy Davies
Design elements by Shutterstock/Nadia Chi
Cover and interior illustrations by Andi Espinosa

978 1 3982 5495 4

British Library Cataloguing in Publication Data
A full catalogue record for this book is available from the British Library.

Printed and bound in India

CONTENTS

DEAD AWAKE

BY BENJAMIN HARPER

I had the craziest dream – one of those dreams that feel so real you know you'll never forget it. It was pitch black. When I tried to move, I couldn't. There was no room. I felt around me and realized I was trapped in a box. The air felt stuffy and damp. It smelled weird, like rotting vegetables. *Gross!* I started squirming, and I punched my way through what felt like a wall.

It was still dark, but I clawed and clawed my way up to what I hoped was going to be fresh air and sunlight.

And then I woke up!

I was so hungry I could barely stand it. I had never felt this hungry before! I needed to eat something, and I needed to eat it NOW. I didn't know exactly what I was craving, but I knew I had to find it fast.

I was out in the street, stumbling around. I don't remember how I got there. In fact, I don't even remember going to bed last night. *Weird.* I was having a hard time moving my legs. They felt stiff, like I had just run a marathon, and my muscles were all clenched up. But this hunger kept me moving forwards.

Food. I needed food right now!

I saw my friend John. I waved and started walking over to him, but he ran away! What had I done to him to make him do that? I was upset. I thought about going after him to ask what was wrong, but then I remembered how hungry I was. *Food. I needed food.*

I rounded the corner onto St James Street and saw some more friends outside the café. When I walked over to them, one of them threw down her doughnut and started screaming! "Hey, don't waste that doughnut!" I wanted to yell at her.

But then the rest of my friends all got up from the table. They turned and looked at me with horror on their faces. And they ran away too!

"They're everywhere!" I heard someone yelling from inside the restaurant. "What are we going to do?"

I ignored her. My friends who had run away left loads of food. Maybe there was something there I could eat.

I walked over to the table. Their plates were piled high with pancakes, scrambled eggs, sausage, bacon, toast, muesli – all sorts of things. But none of it looked good to me. In fact, it all looked . . . disgusting.

I loved bacon! What was the matter with me?

I needed to go home. My mum would be able to help me decide what I wanted to eat. She could help me work out everything else that was going on too, I hoped.

As I walked, people kept running when they saw me. Cars stopped and the people inside stared before speeding off. A dog ran up to me and sniffed me like it had found a tasty snack. I had to push it away because it kept trying to nibble me!

What was going on?

Finally, I got home. I stumbled up the steps but realized I didn't have any keys with me. I tried to lift my arm to ring the doorbell, but it was hard to move. Then, after using all my strength, I managed to push the doorbell.

I heard a noise inside. "Who could that be?" I heard my mum say.

When she opened the door and saw me, she started screaming. She slammed the door in my face. "You can't be here! Go away! What are you?!" I heard her saying from inside.

I banged on the door again.

BANG! BANG! BANG!

I scratched at it. *SCRITCH-SCRATCH!*

I clawed, trying to break it down. I needed to get inside.

I called out to her, but the sounds coming out of my mouth just sounded like groans. I kept trying to speak. "Mum!" I was trying to say. "Mum! I'm hungry!" And then a word finally formed.

"BRAINS!" I heard myself say.

I recognized my voice saying it, but I couldn't work out why. And then I realized . . . I was hungry. I was hungry for BRAINS.

That's when I remembered. That dream wasn't a dream at all. It was real.

I looked at myself in the window of my mother's house. The reflection told me what I already knew. I was no longer alive. Somehow, I was awake and had climbed out of my grave.

And now I was a zombie. And I wanted to eat brains.

"BRAINS!" I cried again, turning away from my mother's house and looking for something to eat.

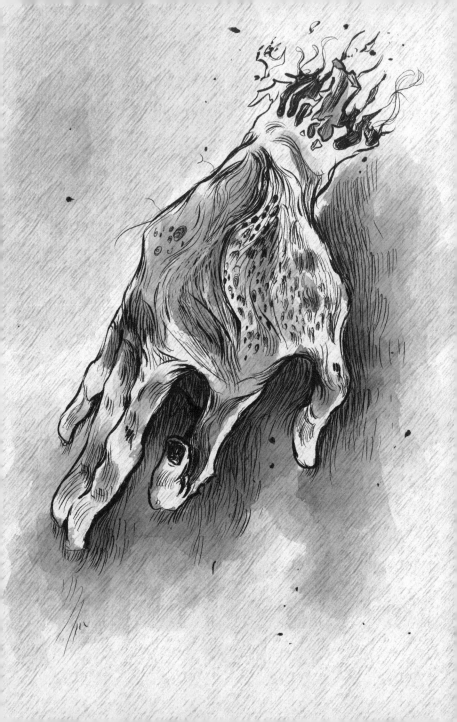

THE ZOMBIE HAND

BY LAURIE S. SUTTON

Thomas Magyar and his son, Richard, drove up
to the old Victorian house that now belonged to
them. It was in the middle of the woods and there
were no houses near by. The run-down house was
gloomy-looking, even in daylight.

Thomas had inherited the house from a relative
he barely knew. The Magyar family had come to this
country from Romania after World War I and spread
from there.

Inside, the house was even gloomier. Dark wood panels covered the walls. Thick velvet curtains hid the windows. The floors creaked like old bones.

Young Richard took a while to explore the house. It was late afternoon when he finally got to the attic. The space was filled with cobwebs and cardboard boxes, but an old trunk caught his eye. It looked like a pirate's treasure chest.

Richard couldn't resist. He opened the chest.

"*Humph.* Nothing but old clothes," Richard said as he picked through them. Then he saw a military uniform.

When Richard lifted the uniform from the chest, a small wooden box fell from its folds. A yellowed envelope was tied to the box with string. But the string was very old and fell apart at Richard's touch.

"Locked," Richard grumbled as he tried to open the box.

The envelope was easy to open though. Richard read the handwritten letter inside.

Never open this box. It contains the hand of a zombie slain in the Carpathian Mountains of Transylvania, in my homeland of Romania, during the War to End All Wars.

I was set upon by the undead monster and only escaped death by chopping the foul creature to pieces. This hand I have taken as a trophy and a reminder of my encounter.

Signed,

Zolta Magyar

"Oh, I've got to see this," Richard murmured.

He dug through the chest looking for a key to the box, but he couldn't find one. He tried to pry off the lock with an old screwdriver he found. But the box stayed sealed. Finally, Richard used the heavy chest itself to smash open the zombie box.

Richard gasped at the sight of a human hand inside the box. It was as pale as a corpse. Bloodless. He picked up the hand and studied it closely.

Suddenly, the thing twitched!

Alarmed, Richard dropped the hand. It landed on the attic floor and stood on its fingers like a spider.

Then it leaped up and grabbed Richard by the throat. It tried to choke him!

Richard clawed the zombie hand from his neck and ran down the stairs. He rushed to find his father, pleading with him to leave. The two fled the house and never returned.

***

A few months later, the new owners of the house arrived. Jan and Tom Durman planned to renovate the place and open a bed-and-breakfast.

On their first night, they sat by the fireplace and talked about what work needed doing. That's when they heard the scratching sounds in the wall.

"Mice," Tom groaned. "I'll get some traps tomorrow."

A familiar shape suddenly darted across the living room floor in the firelight. But it wasn't a mouse. It was the hand. It leaped at Jan's neck.

It took both of them to pull the hand from round her throat. Tom tried to hit it with the metal fireplace poker. Jan grabbed a nearby broom. They chased it round the living room like it was a rabid animal. The whole time, it tried to get its long, bony fingers around their necks. Finally, Tom managed to knock the hand into the fire.

"What was that?" Jan asked.

"I don't know, but the fire will take care of it," Tom replied.

Suddenly, the front door burst open. A man as pale as a corpse stomped into the house. A zombie! He snatched the hand out of the fire and beat out the flames clinging to it. Then, he placed the hand on his wrist. It attached itself perfectly.

"I've been looking for my hand since World War I," the zombie said and wriggled his fingers. "I just didn't know which of Zolta's descendants had it."

"Who . . . what?" Jan stammered.

"Zolta Magyar killed me and chopped me up in 1914. It's taken a long time to get myself back together. He spread my parts all over the place!" the zombie complained. "And now I claim this house as repayment for what he did to me."

Stunned, the Durmans didn't move.

"Leave!" the zombie shouted. "Or I'll eat your brains!"

The Durmans fled the house as the zombie stretched out on the sofa and warmed his chilly corpse by the fire.

ZOMBIE PARK

BY MICHAEL DAHL

The first day of the summer holidays felt like a birthday gift – sunshine, a breeze, just the right temperature and puffy clouds sailing throughout the sky. Leah thought that it couldn't have been a more perfect day. Too bad it didn't stay that way. . .

The morning and afternoon were full of swimming, football, dancing and arguing about which online games to play for the next few months. When evening arrived, Leah and her closest friends didn't want the day to end. So, they sneaked out of their houses and met at the playground in the local park. With little brothers and sisters asleep at home, the place was all theirs.

The giant sandbox of a play area covered half the park. When Leah was younger, she had pretended it was a desert.

The friends were swinging on the swings or sitting on bouncy planes or hanging from the monkey bars. Although a black, moonless sky hung overhead, the sand held heat from the day and kept them comfortably warm.

One of the boys, Oscar, hung from the bars by one hand. "They're called monkey bars," he said to another boy sitting on a bouncy plane.

"It's called a jungle gym," said the boy, Jamie.

"Monkey bars!" Oscar demanded.

"I don't care what you call them. Today was absolutely perfect," said Leah. The gentle drifts of sand made her think of the beach. "Let's go to the lake tomorrow," she said.

A boy called Mark leaned against the monkey bars – he agreed that's what they were called. He shook his head and said, "The lake's closed."

"You can't close a lake," said Leah.

"I mean you can't go swimming there," said Mark. "Because of the zombies."

The friends grew silent. Then Leah moaned. "I thought we were done with zombies."

"Yeah, they're supposed to be gone," whined Nina.

"This happens every time we want to have

fun," said Oscar. He jumped down from the bars. "First there's zombies, then they die out, or the army gets rid of them."

"And then more zombies pop up somewhere else," added Jamie. "It's so annoying!"

"I'm tired of having to stay at home and go to school on the stupid computer," said Leah. The others all agreed.

A shadow appeared by a streetlight in the next street. The figure stopped and looked at the group of friends. Then it ran towards the playground.

"Vincent!" shouted Mark. "Where have you been?"

Vincent was breathing hard. "Zombies," he said. "They found more of them in Anderville."

"Anderville!" Nina shivered. "That's only a few kilometres away. By the zoo."

Vincent nodded. "But the news said they had disappeared. No one knows where they went."

"They're hiding," said Jamie.

Leah looked down at all of the sand. They were surrounded by it. "Do zombies have to breathe?" she asked quietly.

"Of course not," said Oscar. "They're already dead, remember?"

Leah studied the sand beneath the bars. And the sand where they were sitting. Did a small mound just happen to move? Was that her imagination, or was something deadly hidden below?

"Zombies!" she cried. "They're hiding under the sand!" She used to have nightmares about zombies crawling out of the ground – crawling into her house.

The friends were all screaming. They jumped up onto the swings. They crawled to the top of the monkey bars.

"Wait, you guys," said Mark. "Chill. There's no zombies. The sand isn't even moving. Leah's just freaking out."

"Sorry," said Leah.

Nina looked over at the streetlight. "Do you guys hear that?" The sound grew louder and louder. Screeching, howling.

"You said they were by the zoo," Leah said, looking at Nina. "The zoo! Monkey Island. What if zombies bite animals. Can they turn into –?"

Her answer came in a wall of sound. Monkeys were running through the streets. They clambered up the streetlights. The wire fences by the tennis courts were banging back and forth from dozens of monkeys climbing all over them. The friends could see that many of the creatures were missing tails or paws. Hairy little heads were torn apart. Eye sockets were empty.

The friends shouted for help. There was nowhere to run.

Leah looked down at the sand again. She fell to her knees and started digging. She shovelled the sand aside as fast as she could. The others saw her and copied her actions. Sand flew around their heads like a desert storm.

Leah slid into the hole she had made. She buried herself, pulling the loose sand over her chest and legs. Finally, she was covered, with just a hole left to breathe through. Her eyes were shut tight.

Then she waited.

She knew she should have stayed home. She knew it was only a matter of time before she heard the scratching of little paws above her. Little paws digging furiously to find another victim below the monkey bars.

ZOMB-E

BY MEGAN ATWOOD

"Let me see what happens if I make him go into the lake," Jake said, laughing with his new friend, Alex. He moved his video game controller until his character on the screen jumped into the lake. The character jumped in and flailed around. He disappeared below the water, but then he popped back out, spluttering and coughing.

Jake and Alex rolled around laughing.

Jake couldn't believe his luck in getting the brand-new game most people hadn't even heard of yet: *Zomb-E*. Alex had it and had given him a copy. The player got to build and control a zombie character. The best thing about the game, though, was that a player got points if something bad happened to their zombies. Jake hadn't expected it to be so much fun. He couldn't tell his parents about it.

Alex stood up and high-fived Jake. "Tomorrow?" he asked. "Don't play without me!"

Jake nodded and put the controller down. "Sure. See you after school." Jake didn't even know what school Alex went to, but he didn't really care. He wasn't a person to ask too many questions.

Alex left and Jake's sister Sarah came into the room. Jake hurriedly turned off the TV and video game. He didn't think his older sister would like the game either, and with his mum out, she was in charge.

"I'm going to go ride my bike," Jake told her.

Sarah flopped on the sofa and shrugged. "Just stay near by. And come back in an hour." She got on her phone and started texting.

Jake got on his bike. He began pedalling, wondering which direction Alex had gone. Without thinking, he found himself outside his local area. He smiled. His sister and his mum would never know. Jake explored on his bike, giving up on finding Alex and just enjoying seeing something new. He looked to his left and saw that he was by a lake. There was an ambulance and a lot of people standing by the shore. He thought he saw someone lying down by the water's edge, surrounded by paramedics. There was something familiar about all of this.

Jake rode his bike over and listened in to the conversation. He only got snippets: " . . . don't know what happened . . ."

". . . one minute he was talking, the next he was just like a zombie . . ."

Jake put his bike down and moved through the crowd, trying to get a look at the person on the ground. He managed to sneak through and then almost gasped.

The person looked just like his video game character.

The paramedic was saying, "Apparently this guy just jumped in the lake for no reason. Then, even though he's a good swimmer, he got stuck or something. He's lucky to be alive."

Jake felt the blood drain from his face, and he backed away quickly. There was no way it could be his actual character. That couldn't be real. Could it? He thought back to the past few days of playing the game and the things he'd made his character do to get points. It was a crazy idea to think the video game could be real. But just to make sure, he decided to ride around more of this area to see what was happening.

He got back on his bike and began exploring. He passed a house that had been badly burned from the inside out, and he saw people milling about, picking through the debris.

He saw a "No Vacancy" sign on a hotel, and he could see that a huge tree had fallen straight onto the roof.

Both of these things had got him points in the *Zomb-E* game the day before.

He passed two women walking and heard one of them say, "He just lost control of the car, and it kept spinning and spinning until it knocked into a fence by a farm. All the cows got out and now that farmer has gone bankrupt."

He'd done that too.

He rode to the edge of a park with lots of trees and got off his bike. He sat down with his head in his hands and tried to think clearly and calmly about what had happened.

Jake had met Alex a week ago at a park, and they'd hit it off straight away. They were both twelve years old, both really into video games and neither of them had many friends. Alex had come over that same day and brought the *Zomb-E* game. He spent the whole afternoon showing Jake how to play it.

Somehow, this game made things happen in real life. Jake wondered if Alex knew. He headed for home, determined to make things better.

The next day after school, just like it had for a whole week, the doorbell rang. Jake ran to the door and let Alex in.

"Dude," Alex said straight away. "I have to show you this new thing in *Zomb-E*."

Jake didn't say anything as they walked into the living room.

"What's up?" Alex asked, looking confused about Jake's silence.

Jake crossed his arms. "Alex, the things in this video game come true. Did you know that?"

Alex's eyes went wide, and then he shook his head. "That's ridiculous. What are you talking about?"

Jake told him all about his bike ride the day before. And about how all the things he'd done in the game seemed to be happening in real life. Alex's face became more and more surprised.

"That's so weird! But it's just a coincidence," Alex said.

Jake shook his head. "I don't think so, dude," he said.

Then suddenly, Alex's face changed. His eyes

went darker, and he grinned an evil grin. "Okay," he said. Then he flopped down on the sofa and grabbed the controller. "So what?"

Jake couldn't believe his ears. "What do you mean, so what? We're messing with people's lives! We're controlling them like zombies!"

Alex grinned again. "Yeah! What better game could you play?" He sat forwards. "What if we could find people from school? What if we could turn them into zombies too and make them do what we wanted?"

Jake was speechless. But something else burned in his stomach. He thought about all the times he didn't get to sit with anyone at lunch. Or the times he felt left out of people's plans.

"You get points for doing bad stuff, but you can still play even with a bad score. You could also do good stuff," Alex said, his eyes wide and innocent.

Jake thought about that. What if, for every bad thing he did, he also did something good? It would all equal out, right? And then maybe he could finally get his classmates to hang out with him. Or punish them if they didn't . . .

Alex stayed quiet while Jake thought it all through. "Wanna play?" he asked finally.

Jake only hesitated a little bit before he grabbed the controller.

DAY OF THE SCIENCE CLASS DEAD

BY BENJAMIN HARPER

It was that time of year again in Mr Kand's biology class. The day that most kids dreaded. The day with a smell that stayed with you for the rest of your life.

But even though everyone was dreading dissecting dead animals, we never expected the horror of what actually happened on that terrifying day. . .

Mr Kand made us all fill out permission slips to take part in dissecting animals. He said it was an important part of the learning process. It would help us understand how bodies work.

If you ask me, it was just gross. How is looking inside a dead frog supposed to help me understand anything? I mean, we're totally different species.

I had tried to get out of it. "Tell him I'm vegan!" I pleaded with my mum. But she wouldn't budge. "*I* had to do it, so *you* have to too," was her response.

I wanted to scream. I loved animals.

The day arrived, and my lab partner, Gitane, was just as freaked out. But Mr Kand told everyone we needed to behave like adults.

"And anyone who doesn't gets an *F!*" he added. Mr Kand was mean.

There were a few different types of animals to be dissected that day. There were earthworms, frogs, and – for the "lucky" few – pigs. There had been a shortage, so we had to take what we could get, Mr Kand explained.

Everyone was at their lab station getting ready to start. Gitane and I had been given a frog. "At least we didn't get stuck with a pig," she said. "They're so cute."

"Okay, everyone," Mr Kand stated. "Begin."

But just as he said that, there was a bright green flash outside. It filled the room with a near-blinding light. We all covered our eyes. Some kids dived under the lab stations. Others started crying. Rozz shouted, "Finally something interesting is happening!"

The light subsided. We all stared at each other for a minute. The headteacher came in and made an announcement. "Everything is fine, students. It was just a solar flare. Now get back to work."

Whoever heard of a green solar flare? I wasn't buying it. But I didn't have time to think about it for too long.

Kristie was the first to scream.

"It moved! It actually moved!" She jumped up from her station and pushed her animal tray away.

"That's enough nonsense!" Mr Kand shouted, storming over to her station. "See? Nothing's going on here." He was holding up the tray with a frog on it, showing the class. "Now, get back to –"

Work. He was probably going to say work. But he couldn't, because when he opened his mouth, the undead frog jumped off the tray and landed directly on his face.

He pulled it off and threw it across the room. He scrambled back to his desk, where he grabbed a towel and wiped the slime off his face.

"This isn't funny!" he yelled to the class.

But all of a sudden, *all* of the animals started to move. The frogs, pigs and earthworms. The frogs hopped off the trays and onto kids. The pigs jumped down onto the floor, their little trotters clacking on the tiles. And the earthworms just wiggled around.

Then we noticed something. The green glow from the solar flare – it hadn't gone. There was a slow, pulsating green light in the distance.

And when we looked at the pigs and frogs, we saw their eyes were glowing green. They were alive!

The pigs rushed at some students. Their mouths were wide open, and it was pretty obvious that they were going to try to eat us. A pig bit into Lydia's trouser leg. "Get it off! Get it off me!" she screamed, kicking her leg. The pig went flying across the room, but it just got back up and ran again.

The frogs were jumping all over the students, but they didn't have teeth, so they couldn't bite.

They were really trying, though! Kids were pulling frogs off each other and throwing them across the room. But, like the pigs, they just got back up again.

"What are we going to do?" Gitane shouted.

It was clear we all had to get out of the room and into the corridor where it was safe. Mr Kand had a broom, and he got as many kids behind him as he could, swatting off pigs and frogs as we all moved towards the door.

He finally got the entire class behind him as he kept the undead animals at bay with the broom.

"Okay, everyone – run!" he shouted.

Misty was the first out into the corridor. One by one, we all followed, and Mr Kand was the last to leave. He slammed the door shut and locked it.

We saw through the pane of glass on the door that the frogs and pigs were jumping and scratching, trying to get out. The green glow poured in from the outside windows and into the hall. It was so scary, but we were safe!

At least we thought we were.

The pigs and frogs and earthworms, it turns out, were only the beginning.

As we all rushed out of the building, we noticed something else: The green glow was coming from the cemetery across the road. And it looked like there was something happening over there, like something was moving. As it got closer, we realized what it was.

Dozens of zombies were lumbering towards us, their arms up, ready to attack.

"Run!" Mr Kand shouted. But there was nowhere to run. We looked around. We were surrounded.

The Day of the Science Class Dead was far from over.

FRANKENSTEIN'S CAT

BY LAURIE S. SUTTON

The small town of Woodbury had only one vet, but few people took their pets to him. His name was Dr Sheldon "Shelly" Frankenstein, and no one wanted to take their animals to a man with the same name as a mad scientist.

The doctor had turned his garage into an animal hospital. The waiting room in front had only two chairs. The lab and medical equipment were in the back. Instead of pictures of cute animals on the walls, the doctor had posters of the fictional Frankenstein. He was obsessed with the character.

Every night, after office hours, Dr Frankenstein conducted experiments on dead animals. Squirrels. Rats. Sometimes a rabbit. Whatever his cat, Percy, caught around town. The doctor wanted to recreate the science from the Frankenstein story. He wanted to bring life to the lifeless.

"We're a good team," Dr Frankenstein told his cat.

Every night, strange lights and sounds came from the doctor's garage. Neighbours quickened their step as they passed by. Dr Frankenstein had no friends. He didn't mind. He had his cat. He loved Percy very much, and Percy loved him.

One morning, Percy did not wake the doctor up to miaow for breakfast. Dr Frankenstein found him curled up behind the sofa, his favourite hiding place. Sadly, his pet was no longer alive. There was no heartbeat. His little cat body had gone stiff.

"Oh, no! Percy!" the doctor said with tears in his eyes. He stroked his pet's fur gently. "What am I going to do without you?"

That was when Dr Frankenstein decided he would give him life, just like the original Frankenstein character!

The doctor carried Percy to the garage lab. He mixed chemicals together to make a special serum. Then he exposed the cat to radiation using his X-ray machine. He had been close to success in his experiments before. This time he hoped it would finally work for Percy.

"It has to work," Dr Frankenstein said as he injected his pet with the radioactive serum.

But Percy lay still. Minutes went by. Desperate, the doctor grabbed the cardiac paddles and shocked Percy's heart.

The jolt of electricity did the trick! Percy began to breathe.

"Percy!" Dr Frankenstein exclaimed. He picked up his pet and hugged him.

But Percy hissed and squirmed to get away. The doctor was confused. This was not his cat's normal behaviour. Dr Frankenstein finally let go when Percy bit him.

"Ow!" the doctor yelped.

Percy landed on the floor on all fours and ran out of the lab. He escaped from the garage through the cat flap.

"Percy! Come back!" Dr Frankenstein shouted and chased after his pet.

He searched all over town for Percy but couldn't find him. His pet had gone. Sad and tired, the doctor went home, stretched out on the sofa, and fell asleep.

It was the next morning when Dr Frankenstein woke up. He wondered why he was on the sofa. Then he remembered. Percy was dead. Then he came to life again. Then he ran away.

"I should be excited that my experiment worked," the doctor said. "But it's not the same without Percy."

Dr Frankenstein got up and went to the kitchen to make breakfast. He poured some cereal in a bowl but pushed it away. He suddenly had a powerful craving for something else. He knew he didn't have what he wanted in the house. He had to find it.

It took a trip to a butcher's shop for the doctor to finally find what he hungered for. He came home with several cow brains and gobbled them up. After a feeding frenzy, Dr Frankenstein sat back with a full stomach. Now he could think about what had happened.

"I ate brains. All I want to eat is brains. Am I . . . a zombie?" Dr. Frankenstein wondered. "But how? I didn't get bitten by a zombie."

Then he remembered his cat, Percy.

"My experiment must have turned Percy into a zombie!" the doctor realized. "Then he bit me and turned me into one too."

Dr Frankenstein went online and ordered a large supply of gourmet cow brains to be delivered to his home. Then he went to his garage lab.

"Percy isn't coming back to me," the doctor said. "But I can make another pet."

Dr Frankenstein started to put together parts of a rabbit and a squirrel. Soon he had created a whole new animal. The lights and sounds started up again in Dr Frankenstein's garage lab.

Outside, in the dead of night, a zombie cat prowled through the town . . .

ZOMBIE PET CLUB

BY MICHAEL DAHL

"Mum! Dad! She's here!" Kimmie Taylor jumped up and down, pointing out of the window.

Mum and Dad smiled. "The headteacher said in his letter that she'd be home by six o'clock, and it's exactly that now," said Mum.

A school bus hissed its brakes, stopping in front of the Taylors' front garden. On the side of the bus were the letters ZISD. Zombie Independent School District. As Kimmie ran to see her older sister, she noticed that some neighbours had gathered outside.

They stood in small groups, crossing their arms, whispering, pointing. One of them spat on the side of the bus as if the black letters were crawling snakes.

The doors wheezed open. Serena Taylor walked down the steps onto the grass.

Mr and Mrs Taylor ran over and gave their daughter a big hug. "Oh, Serena, we missed you!" said Dad. "You'll have to tell us all about the exchange programme. And your new, uh, family." Mum was crying and smiling. She glanced up from her handkerchief and noticed the neighbours. Some of them were still staring. Others had turned round, with their backs to the happy family.

Kimmie took Serena's hand. "C'mon, we need to eat. Mum made a special dinner, and there's cake!"

Mum and Dad hurried the girls inside. As the bus pulled away, two or three of its windows snapped open. Dark eyes within watched the Taylors walk into their house. "Goodbye, Serena, goodbye," hollow voices rang out. Several arms stuck out of the windows and waved to Serena. The arms were blue and grey. Hands were missing fingers. One of the neighbours saw this and screamed.

Inside the house, Dad grabbed Serena's backpack and suitcase. Her mother looked closely at the girl. "You alright, honey?" she asked. "You look pale. And skinny! Didn't they feed you at that school?"

"She just misses her friends," suggested Kimmie.

Mum nodded. "You're probably right," she said.

"Gus and Fluffy missed you," said Kimmie, referring to their dog and cat.

"I put your things in your old bedroom. Did I tell you that we are so proud of you?" said Dad. "Not every girl can live with zombies for a whole school year."

Serena was quiet and polite. She sat in her old chair at the dinner table. Mum set a plate in front of her. "Just the way you like it – chicken salsa meatloaf."

The girl's cheeks grew paler. Her eyes were sad.

Mum bit her lip. "Don't worry. It may take some time to get back to your normal life."

There was a loud knock at the door. "We don't answer the door at dinnertime," yelled Kimmie. At the next bold knock, Serena sat up. For the first time that night, she had energy. She popped up from the table. "I'll get it," she said.

Serena opened the door. Her parents tried hard not to gasp out loud. Kimmie's eyes grew wide. Four girls stood at the door. Each carried a lunch box, pink, yellow or mint green. They giggled and smiled at Serena. "Is this too early?" asked one of the girls without a nose. Zombie girls, thought Kimmie.

Serena waved the girls inside. She turned to her parents at the dinner table. "I'm sorry," she said brightly. "I asked some of the girls in my club to visit. Is this alright?"

"Of course," said Mum. "Your friends are always welcome."

"They came early because they can't stay out late," explained Serena. "The fence closes, you know."

"Do your friends want dinner?" asked Dad. The four visitors giggled again.

"We brought our own snacks," said one of the girls. She jiggled her pink lunch box.

"Come on," said Serena. The Taylors' dog, Gus, started barking from the utility room, where he was kept during dinner. "Don't worry," said Serena. "That's just my dog I told you about."

"Yes!" said the girl with the missing nose. "Pets are the best."

The girls followed Serena down the hallway and disappeared into her bedroom. The door clicked.

"At least she has friends," said Mum.

In a few minutes, Gus started barking again. "I'll go and see him," said Kimmie.

She got up from the table and opened the utility room door. But Gus was missing. Kimmie made a beeline for Serena's door. Her sister had locked it, but from experience, Kimmie knew she could peek through the old-fashioned keyhole.

All the girls were sitting on Serena's bed. One of them said, "I call this meeting of the Pet Club to order." They all clapped.

"Should we talk about our summer plans," asked another, "or talk about our pets while we snack?"

"Pets!" they all said.

Kimmie watched the girls open their lunches.

Then she had to stop. She stood back from the keyhole and covered her mouth. *What a Pet Club!* thought Kimmie. Serena's friends were eating parts of their pets for dinner. But at least Serena – oh no! She patted the pillow next to her and Gus jumped up, his tail wagging. That's why Gus started barking again, thought Kimmie.

Serena opened her mouth. Her teeth were sharper than her little sister remembered.

"Mum! Dad! She's gonna eat the dog!" shouted Kimmie. "She's a zombie!"

She turned round and saw her parents already standing behind her. "Yes, dear, we know," said Mum. "Serena has changed since she went to the new school. She's growing up. And her headteacher wrote that she won't hurt anyone in the family. Probably. So she needs our support, right?"

Dad looked over at Kimmie. "Honey, can you go and get the cat?"

DEAD EYES

BY MEGAN ATWOOD

Mohammed looked down at the big *D* grade on his maths test. Tears welled up in his eyes. Another bad maths grade. He'd have to show his parents tonight – they always asked. And he'd have to watch his father's face drop with disappointment. As an engineer, Mohammed's father thought that Mohammed should be good at maths. Mohammed agreed. But he wasn't.

Mohammed looked up at Mr Patterson, not hearing a word he said. The boy blinked his eyes to clear the tears. The last thing Mohammed wanted to do was cry at school.

Mr Patterson stood at the board, writing an equation. Mohammed realized the teacher was going over the test, so he flipped over his paper again. Maybe if he could work out what he did wrong. . . . When he glanced up again, he gasped so loudly that other kids turned to look at him.

He didn't care. Floating beside Mr Patterson's head were two dead-looking red eyes, glaring at him. *Zombie eyes!* Mohammed thought.

Mohammed looked around in confusion – no one else seemed to notice the dead eyes. "Um," he said. Sniggers erupted around him, and Mohammed could feel the blood rushing to his face.

Luckily, the bell rang and Mohammed looked down at his paper again. When he looked up, the zombie eyes had gone. He shook his head to clear his mind. Clearly, he was now hallucinating.

When Mohammed got home, he flicked his shoes off at the door and called for his mum, stuffing the maths test in his backpack. If he stuck it deep enough in a pocket, maybe he could pretend it didn't exist.

His mum came out in her nurse's uniform and gave him a hug. She tilted his chin up and searched his face. "Hard day?" she asked. As she said it, something red flashed behind her head. Mohammed looked around her.

Zombie eyes. Staring at him.

Mohammed stared straight into the dead eyes, hoping to blink them away. They blinked back at him. He looked around the room and saw his cat grooming herself in the window. As he watched, another pair of zombie eyes blinked into existence just above the cat. And then to his horror, his little sister skipped down the stairs and Mohammed watched as a pair of red, menacing eyes followed right behind her.

His knees went weak. "I have . . ." he said, then ran past all the red eyes up into his bedroom, slamming the door harder than he meant to.

He sat on his bed and willed his legs to stop shaking. "They are just eyes," he said to himself. "Eyes can't do anything." But the picture in his mind still terrified him. Mohammed could just feel that these eyes meant something bad.

He flipped open his laptop and did some research. His parents called him down for supper. He begrudgingly went, but the eyes were everywhere around his family. So he shovelled down some food and sprinted back up the stairs to hop back on his computer. After a couple of hours, he found it: a website called ZOMBIE EYES, of all things. Mohammed pored over the information. Evidently, this could be common for school kids having a tough time with something. Mohammed thought of his *D*. He was having a tough time with something alright. He kept reading and saw that there was an answer: Draw Xs on 3/5ths of the windows in the house, then chant a phrase at midnight.

Mohammed smiled. He could do that.

Exactly at midnight, Mohammed enacted the plan from the website. He drew Xs on 3/5ths of the windows in his house – he was pretty sure he had that right – and chanted the phrase, "Dead eyes go, I will stay. Keep your menacing looks at bay," over and over again. When he was satisfied he'd said it enough times, he went to bed.

The next morning, he went down to breakfast. His dad was at the cooker and his mother and sister sat together at the kitchen table. "Good morning," Mohammed called, as he picked up a glass for orange juice.

His dad turned round and his mum and sister looked up. Mohammed dropped the glass. Every one of them had glowing red eyes. They were zombies! He sprinted out of the house, but it didn't get better: every person he saw had dead-looking, red eyes.

As he ran, he realized: 3/5ths of the windows. He must have done the maths wrong. Again.

GLOSSARY

CARDIAC having to do with the heart

CORPSE dead body

EQUATION mathematical statement that one set of numbers or values is equal to another set of numbers or values

EXISTENCE living, or having a reality

INHERIT receive money or property from someone who died

PARAMEDIC person trained to give medical treatment in an emergency

PULSATING beating or vibrating regularly

RABID extremely violent

RADIATION particles that are sent out of a radioactive substance

SERUM liquid used to prevent or cure a disease

SUBSIDE become less intense or active

DISCUSSION QUESTIONS

1. What is your favourite story in this book? Discuss why you liked that particular story so much.
2. What makes a scary story so creepy? Talk about two or three things (blood, zombies, ghosts or other) that scare your socks off!
3. Discuss some of the different ways in which zombies were portrayed in these stories. How were they different? How were they similar? Use examples from the book.

WRITING PROMPTS

1. Write another zombie story. How will you make your story different from the ones included in this book?
2. Write a second part, or sequel, to one of the stories in this book. What happens next? You decide!
3. Create a list of your biggest fears, such as spiders, zombies or the dark. Then write down how you might be able to overcome these fears.

ABOUT THE AUTHORS

MEGAN ATWOOD

Megan Atwood is a writer and professor with over 45 books published. She lives in New Jersey, USA, where she wrangles cats, dreams up ridiculous stories and thinks of ways to make children laugh all day.

MICHAEL DAHL

Michael Dahl is the prolific author of more than 200 books for children and young adults. He has won the AEP Distinguished Achievement Award three times for his non-fiction, a Teacher's Choice award from *Learning* magazine and a Seal of Excellence from the Creative Child Awards. Dahl currently lives in Minneapolis, Minnesota, USA.

BENJAMIN HARPER

Benjamin Harper lives in Los Angeles, USA, where he edits superhero books for a living. When he's not at work, he writes, watches horror films and hangs out with his cats Marjorie and Jerry, a betta fish called Toby and a tank full of four rough-skinned newts. He tends a bog garden full of carnivorous plants and also grows milkweed to help save Monarch butterflies. His other books include the Bug Girl series, *Obsessed With Star Wars*, *Star Wars: Rolling with BB-8!*, *Hansel & Gretel & Zombies* and many more.

LAURIE S. SUTTON

Laurie Sutton is a comic book writer and editor. She is also the author of *The Mystery of the Aztec Tomb* and *The Secret of the Sea Creature* from the You Choose Stories: Scooby-Doo! series. She currently lives in Florida, USA.

READ ALL FOUR